Murder in the Quiet Hours

A Little Firling Mystery – Book Nine

by Belinda Chavremootoo

Dedication

For every cat who ever solved a mystery quietly before the humans caught up. Especially for one.

Text Copyright

First Edition

Table of Contents

Prologue

Then.

The clock on the wall ticked too loudly.

02:17.

The fluorescent light above the doorway buzzed faintly, the sound barely louder than the shallow breaths that came from the hospital bed.

She was old. That much was clear. Her hands — curled gently over the edge of the blanket — were thin, pale, with paper-soft skin.

But she had been *talking yesterday*.

Her daughter had come. Brought grapes. They'd laughed, hadn't they?

She wasn't supposed to go yet.

The door opened with a whisper.

Someone stepped in — soft shoes. A figure in pale blue scrubs. No rush, no clipboard, no sound except for the careful pull of gloves.

The woman in the bed stirred slightly.

"Shhh," said the voice, calm and kind.

"You've done enough now."

A cool hand touched her forehead.

"You can rest."

She didn't resist. She couldn't.

The monitor gave a soft tone — a single beep — then silence. Flatline.

The figure stood there for a moment longer, watching.

Then turned off the monitor, wiped the gloves clean, and left the room — without a trace.

The hallway outside was still. No alarms. No voices.

Just quiet.

Too quiet.

Chapter 1

The mornings had started to bite.

Annabel wrapped her scarf tighter as she stepped out of Honeystone Cottage, Persephone trotting ahead like a queen who expected the world to rise when she passed.

The trees along the lane had begun to turn — gold and copper leaves tangled in their own descent. The air smelled of damp earth, and the sky was that soft grey that never really chose a mood.

"Don't charm the doctors too quickly," Annabel murmured to the cat.

"Let them think I'm the one who signed the volunteer form."

Persephone flicked her tail like she didn't appreciate the slander.

***

The hospital smelled of antiseptic and over-washed sheets.

There was noise at the reception desk — phones, keyboards, the soft shuffle of heels — but deeper inside, the corridors hushed. Not in reverence, but in routine.

The kind of quiet that settled in long ago and never left. Monitors beeped softly behind closed doors.

A cart of meal trays clattered too loudly as it turned a corner too fast, and a nurse swore gently under her breath before righting it.

Annabel was guided to the children's ward — a sun-painted corridor filled with faded kites and lopsided butterflies.

The soft hum of an aquarium echoed down the hall, its light casting green shimmer onto the linoleum floor.

"They're a mixed bunch," said the nurse. "Recovering surgeries, some with autoimmune disorders. One or two oncology cases. Ages six to twelve, mostly. Bright as anything."

Annabel nodded, fingers tightening slightly on the book in her hand.

***

Back in the village, Evie had been the one to push her into this.

"You need purpose," she'd said.

"Or at least someone small and sticky to ask you strange questions about frogs."

She hadn't said *why* she was so certain.

But earlier that morning, Annabel had passed her in the bookshop — Evie holding a framed photo, half-dusted. A woman in her fifties smiled from beneath a sunhat, surrounded by foxgloves.

Evie hadn't spoken. Just set it back on the mantle a little too carefully.

"She died this time of year," she'd said after a moment.

"Every fall smells like her garden."

***

The children embraced her like they'd been waiting all week. A boy with a bandaged leg offered her his blanket. A girl with a shaved head showed her the stuffed rabbit she'd named after the hospital janitor. One with braces on both legs asked if Persephone *ate books.*

Persephone blinked at him and nestled into his lap like she'd always lived there.

Annabel read two stories, then one more.

It felt… good.

Strange, but good. A kind of peace she hadn't expected to find again.

***

Later, as they walked back through the hallway, a trolley of linens rushed past, rattling too fast, too loud. Annabel stepped aside, and a nurse murmured a quick apology.

And then, just as they reached the doors to the lift, a quiet voice behind them said:

"You've got a lovely way with them."

Annabel turned, but no one was there.

Just silence.

And the soft beep of a monitor behind a half-open door.

***

Outside, the air was crisp and dusky, the scent of autumn leaves curling in the wind. Persephone leapt into the passenger seat of the car without protest — her weekly ride back from what she clearly considered *"her audience."*

Annabel smiled faintly as she started the engine.

"You're becoming quite the celebrity," she murmured.

But the smile faded as her thoughts drifted back — not to the children laughing or listening or asking absurd questions — but to the two she hadn't seen today. One had been transferred. The other… she wasn't told.

And there was something about the room across the hallway — that monitor tone.

The *flatness of it.*

She shook it off.

But not all the way.

***

She didn't know when the hospital visits had become a rhythm — or why she'd come to need them. She told herself it was about giving something back. *Finding structure. Balance.*

But there was more to it.

Those children, especially the ones with the thinnest wrists and bravest eyes — *they lived harder in a single hour than some adults did in a lifetime.*

And Persephone? She knew.

She curled against the weakest ones. Nuzzled the scared ones.

And she always looked back over her shoulder before they left — like she was making sure nothing stayed behind that shouldn't.

Chapter 2

That night, Evie came for dinner.

The kitchen at Honeystone Cottage was warm and full of rosemary and slow-roasted vegetables. Persephone wound between chairs like a furry satellite. The fire crackled in the grate, low and soft.

"You're spoiling me," Evie said, shrugging off her coat.

"I was fully prepared for tea and toast."

"You get soup, fresh bread, and second-hand affection from my cat," Annabel replied. "Accept your blessings."

They ate quietly at first. A soft kind of quiet. Comfortable. Familiar.

"How was today?" Evie asked finally, reaching for another slice of bread.

Annabel told her about the girl who wanted to be an astronaut, and the boy who asked if she could bring books about dragons next time. She didn't mention the empty bed. Or the monitor.

"It's strange," she said at last. "I didn't think I'd feel… needed."

"They do that to you," Evie murmured. "Kids. They make you want to try harder."

There was a beat of silence, then Evie picked up her wine glass, turning it between her hands.

"My aunt used to say children were the only ones honest enough to tell you what you are."

"She once told me I was a wild weed with too many thorns."

"Then she handed me gardening gloves and said to make peace with myself."

Annabel watched her carefully.

"You were close."

"She was the only one who wanted me." Evie blinked, quickly. "The only one who didn't expect me to be someone else."

"It's been…" she trailed off. "Ten years this week."

Annabel reached for the bottle, refilling her glass. Persephone leapt softly into Evie's lap, as if she'd been listening the whole time.

"She'd like that you remember her with wine," Annabel said gently.

Evie smiled. "She liked her reds."

Then quieter: "I wonder what she'd think of me now."

Outside, the wind picked up. A single leaf hit the window with a soft, papery sound.

Chapter 3

The following Wednesday, Annabel returned to the hospital with a new tote bag — dragons, as promised — and a small knitted crown Persephone had promptly tried to destroy.

The air was damp and heavy, the smell of rain still clinging to the bricks. Inside, the hospital corridors felt warmer than usual, as though the heating had kicked in a touch too early.

In the children's ward, Nora — the quiet girl with the stargazing eyes — wasn't there.

"Transferred?" Annabel asked casually, pulling out her book.

The nurse paused. Just for a second.

"Moved to another ward," she said. "Might be going home soon."

Annabel nodded, but her hand stilled against the page.

Something in the phrasing didn't feel like celebration.

It felt like avoidance.

***

The children were quieter that day. Clingier. Less giggles, more hand-holding. Persephone weaved between them, curling beside a boy with an IV line and licking his knuckles like she was trying to clean away something only she could smell.

"She's gotten very serious," one nurse joked gently. "Like a little doctor in fur."

Annabel smiled, but it didn't quite reach her eyes.

***

Later, on her way out, she passed a whiteboard in the corridor she hadn't noticed before. It listed birthdays, welcome messages, and a small note about *Nora's discharge*.

It was scribbled hastily. The handwriting was different.

And where the nurse's name should have been signed… it had simply been crossed out.

***

That evening, back at Honeystone Cottage, she poured herself a glass of wine and curled up on the sofa, Persephone at her feet. She reached into her bag for the hospital's weekly thank-you flyer — little drawings from the children, volunteer updates.

But as she unfolded the paper, her eyes caught on a list of patient transfers.

No Nora.

Not under children's.

Not under general.

Not under oncology.

She checked twice. Then again.

It could have been a mistake.

Or maybe it meant nothing at all.

But something settled into her stomach like fog.

She didn't know what yet.

Only that she would be *paying closer attention next week.*

Chapter 4

The market in Little Firling smelled of wet leaves, cinnamon rolls, and gossip.

Annabel balanced her wicker basket on one arm, a mental list ticking over as she reached for coriander seeds and refilled her dwindling jar of sumac. The stallholder — a cheery man in a knitted jumper with a beetroot stain — greeted her with his usual wink.

"Back to the hospital today?" he asked.

"Yesterday," she said. "They've started calling Persephone 'Doctor Paws.'"

"Should be the one prescribing cat cuddles for the whole ward," he grinned. "Better than the lot they've got."

She smiled politely, but she was distracted.

Further down the lane, near the vegetable carts, two older women were talking softly beside baskets of late-season plums and bruised apples.

"—didn't even get to say goodbye," one was saying.

"They said it was peaceful. Just… went in the night."

"That's the third one this month."

Annabel didn't mean to listen.

But her hands stilled over a bundle of rosemary.

And her ears tuned in before she told them to.

"Which ward was it?"

"Palliative, I think. Or maybe general. You know how it is with them."

She moved on quickly, but the words followed her down the row of stalls.

***

At the apothecary counter, she ran into Miss Tamsin from the charity shop, who was carefully selecting cough drops and loose-leaf chamomile.

"I heard about the little girl," she said softly.

"Nora? My niece volunteers at the desk — said she passed last week. Heartbreaking."

Annabel blinked.

"I thought she'd been discharged."

"No, no," said Tamsin. "Wasn't her time, poor thing. But they said it was peaceful. One of the night staff found her asleep. Just… never woke up."

***

Annabel drove home slowly.

She didn't know what she was thinking exactly.

Just that *discharged* and *dead* were not synonyms.

And that someone, somewhere… had lied.

Chapter 5

Annabel returned to the hospital the following Wednesday with a fresh copy of *The Secret Garden* tucked in her bag and a pouch of cat treats Persephone had been known to demand mid-story.

She wasn't sure if it was the colder weather or her own mood, but the hallways felt dimmer that day. Or maybe just quieter.

As she reached the volunteer desk, a familiar voice stopped her in her tracks.

"So, you didn't see the turn?"

"No, sir. It all happened so fast. I remember the dog barking, and then…"

Tom Oakes stood at the corner of the corridor, notebook in hand, speaking gently to a man in a wrist brace and a scuffed jacket.

"Tom?" she said, approaching.

He looked up, surprised.

"Annabel! What are you doing here?"

"Reading to the kids. You?"

"Just routine — small incident, nothing criminal. He fell into a ditch trying to get his dog back from the road. Lucky it wasn't worse."

The man gave a small wave with his good hand. "Wasn't the dog's fault," he muttered. "Just... lost in my head."

"You alright?" Annabel asked gently.

"Sort of. It's been a bad few weeks."

"Family?" she asked, and regretted it immediately.

He nodded, eyes dropping.

"My niece passed away here. Nora. You might've seen her."

Annabel froze.

Tom looked between them, eyebrows lifting.

"You knew her?"

"I read to her," Annabel said slowly. "But I was told she'd been discharged."

"No," said the man. "They said it was peaceful. That she passed in her sleep. But… it doesn't feel real. She was doing better, you know?"

He wiped at his face quickly.

"They said it just… happened."

***

Annabel didn't know what to say.

Tom gave her a look as the man was guided gently away by a nurse.

"You alright?" he asked softly.

"I'm not sure," she replied. "I think I've been told different versions of the same story."

"Doesn't mean anything's wrong," he said.

"No," she agreed. "But it's…
unusual."

Chapter 6

It was Evie who brought it up.

They were walking back from the post office, arms full of brown-wrapped book deliveries and fresh gossip, when she paused in front of the old noticeboard outside the village hall.

"Oh," she said. "That's sad."

A new funeral notice had been posted — simple, handwritten, pinned with a gold thumbtack.

"Glenda Marsh. 74. Passed peacefully at Little Firling Hospital. No known next of kin."

Annabel frowned. "She lived in Little Yewling, didn't she?"

"Up near the apple orchard. Always wore those massive earrings." Evie tilted her head. "She used to help with the village fete. Bit of a firecracker."

"Any family?"

"Just a cousin, I think. But they don't speak. There was some row about a will years ago. Glenda lived alone."

"Was she unwell?"

Evie paused.

"Not that I know of. She had trouble with her hip, but I thought she was getting better. Broke it in a fall last month, but I ran into her just last week. She said she was being discharged soon. Couldn't wait to get home to her hydrangeas."

Annabel stared at the notice again.

"No funeral arrangements listed."

"Probably council-handled," Evie said quietly. "No one left to plan it."

***

They walked the rest of the way in silence, except for the crunch of leaves underfoot.

Back at the shop, Annabel helped Evie sort new arrivals. But the title of one book — *The Still Hours* — stuck in her head.

They were all alone.

They were getting better.

And they died.

***

That night, she started a list.

She didn't know why.

She just… wrote down the names she'd heard over the past month.

Nora. Glenda.

The man at the market's sister.

And the woman from the café whose uncle "just slipped away."

She stared at it for a long time.

Just names.

But *somehow, together… they felt like a pattern.*

Chapter 7

The parish registrar's office sat behind the Little Firling library, next to a broken radiator and a shelf of half-finished jigsaw puzzles. It smelled faintly of damp paper, vanilla tea, and the slow sigh of time.

Annabel signed in with her usual neat script.

Prue at the desk didn't ask why.

She knew Annabel — former professor, bookstore co-owner, longtime volunteer — and she'd been seen doing odder things for research over the years.

"Hospital deaths, last few months?" Prue asked, already pulling out the folder.

"Not many lately. Still, life keeps its own calendar, doesn't it?"

Annabel offered a neutral smile.

"Just looking through. Something's been on my mind."

***

She took the records to a quiet table beneath the window, where the afternoon light softened the edges of the page.

She wasn't sure what she expected to find.

She told herself this was about tying up loose thoughts.

But she had *too many of those lately.*

***

The register was tidy. Each page handwritten with practiced form. Details registered were name, dates of birth and death, place of death, the name of the informant and the cause of death.

But after half an hour, she noticed *four entries* that didn't sit quite right.

***

The first one was for Nora Hensley, aged 9 died of natural causes and her death informed by the ward sister.

Annabel remembered Nora's bright smile, her plans to become a vet. The staff had said she was doing well.

The second entry was that of Glenda Marsh, aged 74 and died of cardiac arrest but the informant was missing. Evie said she was improving. Was meant to be discharged that week.

The third entry was that of Morris Elford, aged 81 with no next of kin with cause of death as *"Pending coroner's review"*. Annabel wondered why the cause was still pending since it had been six weeks.

Finally, the fourth case was that of Dorothy Combs, aged 88 and the staff nurse reported her death.

But the name of the nurse was written over correction tape. Beneath it, something faintly scribbled out. All four died without their family being present in the early hours.

Three died between 2:10 and 4:00 a.m. at Little Firling Hospital. It wasn't the number but the *repetition of conditions* that made Annabel uncomfortable.

***

Annabel copied the entries carefully into her notebook. She wasn't jumping to conclusions — she never did. But something about the shape of the data made her pause.

"They were supposed to be getting better."

She didn't know if that was true for every name.

But she knew it was for Nora.

And Evie had sworn it was for Glenda.

And she remembered how Persephone had curled beside Nora that day, quiet and still.

Like she'd already known.

***

She closed the book gently and returned it to the desk.

"All done?" Prue asked, adjusting her mushroom earrings.

"For today," Annabel replied, slipping her notebook into her coat. "I might be back."

"Anything interesting?"

Annabel paused.

"I'm not sure yet. But… something feels off."

"Funny how we always say that when the leaves start turning," Prue chuckled.

Annabel smiled faintly, but it didn't quite reach her eyes.

Outside, the wind chased a swirl of gold leaves down the pavement like secrets fleeing just out of reach.

Chapter 8

Annabel brought shortbread.

It never hurt.

The Suffolk District Coroner's Office handled deaths from Little Firling and the surrounding villages — small places didn't have their own coroner.

The main facility was tucked behind a row of business units and had the sterile echo of places meant to feel efficient rather than comforting.

Inside, the floors gleamed with pale vinyl, the walls a clean blue-grey. No clutter. No carpet.

The faint scent of antiseptic drifted beneath the hum of overhead lights.

Layla Shaw, the coroner's assistant, met her at the door with a clip-on badge and a glance that said she was both curious and very slightly concerned.

"You again," she said, half-smiling. "Trouble magnet."

"Professional curiosity," Annabel replied, lifting the tin.

"And a bribe."

"Shortbread diplomacy. Come on in."

Layla tapped her card to unlock the inner doors.

"Jameson's in," she added over her shoulder.

"He's been low-key grumbling about a file you're probably here to talk about."

***

The conference room was minimalist: polished steel table, two chairs, no clutter. A file tray sat perfectly aligned to one side. Even sound felt thinner here — like words had to walk carefully.

Persephone remained in her carrier near Annabel's feet, ears twitching with every echo of movement.

Dr. Jameson entered with a black coffee and his usual air of crisp detachment.

"Dr. Deighton," he greeted, using the title with his usual measured formality. "What string are you tugging this time?"

"Just one that didn't feel quite knotted."

"Morris Elford?" he asked, lowering himself into the chair across from her.

"Six weeks. Cause of death still pending."

He nodded. "Technically natural causes. But the paperwork wasn't complete — the attending nurse hadn't signed the final meds chart, and the timing was… unexpected."

"Unexpected in what way?"

"He was stable. Due for discharge within the week."

Layla folded her arms. "So, we flagged it. Asked for the full treatment chart, medication schedule, and a witness statement."

"Is that standard?" Annabel asked.

"Not always," Jameson replied. "But when a patient dies overnight, unattended, and wasn't considered palliative, we need to be thorough. Especially when no next of kin is available to raise concern."

Annabel nodded slowly.

"That's the thing," she said. "It's not just Morris. I've seen four other cases. Similar time of death — early morning. Most without family. One had a discharge scheduled. One had no informant listed at all."

Jameson sipped his coffee. "You think it's a pattern?"

"I think it's more than coincidence. Possibly a procedural issue. Possibly malpractice."

"Not murder?" Layla asked, quiet but direct.

"I don't know enough yet to use that word," Annabel said. "But the pattern hums."

Jameson looked down at her notes. He didn't smile, but there was the faintest flicker of something like professional appreciation.

"We've seen care homes cover missteps before," he said. "And hospital corners get cut. It's easier when no one's watching. Easier still when the patients have no one waiting."

Layla murmured, "You think this might be… deliberate?"

"No," Jameson said. "But I think something's off. And we're overdue for a closer look."

***

As Annabel stood to leave, Persephone let out a low, unimpressed trill from her carrier.

Jameson tilted his head. "You're bringing her to autopsy now?"

"She's an emotional support professional," Annabel replied. "Part-time philosopher."

Layla grinned. "We'll let you know what we find."

"Thank you," Annabel said. "For listening."

Jameson gave a small nod, eyes sharper now.

"Let us know if any more names start humming."

Chapter 9

It was a rare quiet evening at Honeystone Cottage.

Annabel had made a mushroom risotto — earthy, comforting — and Evie had brought a bottle of Rioja with a label she'd mostly picked for its bold font.

The fire crackled in the hearth, and Persephone dozed on the rug like a lazy sphinx, her tail flicking now and then at dreams only she knew.

They talked about unremarkable things at first — books, village gossip, the awful new display at the grocers. But something in Annabel's voice had carried tension all night. Not worry, exactly. But *heaviness.*

When they'd moved to the sofa and the wine had warmed them both, Annabel spoke.

"Evie… do you remember much about your aunt's last week?"

Evie's fingers tensed around the stem of her glass. She didn't look up right away.

"Not much," she said finally. "I try not to."

"I was looking into some hospital records," Annabel continued gently. "And something didn't sit right. Not about your aunt specifically — just a pattern."

Evie didn't answer immediately. She took a long sip of wine, then set the glass down with a little more force than necessary.

"She was doing better," she said. "That's what they told me. Said she was cranky and asking to go home. Making jokes."

"Do you remember who told you?"

"A nurse, I think. Over the phone. I wasn't here — I'd gone to Brighton for a story. Flooding, or something dramatic that didn't actually happen. At that time, I was working as a journalist."

She exhaled, short and sharp.

"They called and said she'd passed in her sleep. Said it was peaceful. Unexpected, but… peaceful."

"Did you see her chart? Talk to a doctor?"

"No. It was already done by the time I got there."

Annabel reached out and placed a hand over hers.

"You don't need to feel guilty—"

"But I do," Evie cut in, voice tight. "Because she was *alone*. Because she made me promise to be back Thursday and she died on *Wednesday night*."

Silence fell for a moment, broken only by the pop of the firewood.

"I remember the nurse saying, *'It surprised us too.'* And I thought… why didn't I ask what that meant?"

***

Persephone jumped up onto the armrest and pressed her head against Evie's shoulder.

Evie stroked her absently, her eyes somewhere far away.

"She wasn't dying," she whispered. "She was *getting better.*"

Annabel's mind clicked quietly through her mental file.

One more name. One more story.

One more *death that wasn't expected.*

"Do you remember the name of the nurse?" she asked softly.

Evie shook her head. "No badge. No name. Just… tired eyes and a soft voice."

"Would you be willing to let me look into it?"

Evie hesitated.

Then, slowly, she nodded.

"If there's even the smallest chance…" she said, voice cracking just slightly, "that something's been happening — and I never asked the right questions—"

"Then let's ask them now," Annabel said.

Chapter 10

It was nearly midnight when the message arrived.

From: *Layla Shaw*

Subject: *RE: Quiet Query*

Body:

Annabel,

I didn't want to put this in the system notes. But I thought you should know — Morris Elford's PM file came back from the hospital review. There's a note in the margin of his initial triage: "Mobility improving, vitals stable, BP managed."

No mention of any change in condition before the time of death. In fact,

the attending doctor had marked
"discharge likely within 48 hours."
Sound familiar?
– L.

Annabel sat back from her laptop. The room was dark except for the lamplight and Persephone's eyes reflecting back at her like twin moons.

Yes.

It sounded very familiar.

***

The next morning, Annabel walked into the Little Firling Hospital under the soft pretext of visiting — one of the regulars from the children's ward had gone home, but she'd promised to bring back a favourite book just in case he returned for check-ups.

She brought pastries. She brought smiles.

Evie has not wanted to come.

"It's not that I don't care," she said, folding her arms tightly. "It's that I still can't walk through those doors without seeing the bed."

Annabel didn't push. She never did.

"I understand," she said gently. "Would you mind if I asked about her? Just the room, the timing. Nothing confidential."

Evie hesitated, then nodded once.

"She was in Room 304. Orthopaedic wing. Name was Constance Caldwell. They said she was being discharged on Thursday."

A pause.

"She died Wednesday night."

***

Annabel asked after a few of the children she'd read to, lingered near the volunteer board, and then approached the front desk with her calmest voice.

"My friend's aunt passed here a couple of years ago," she said. "We're trying to piece together a few things from that time — nothing medical, I promise. Just memory."

The receptionist raised an eyebrow but nodded politely.

"Do you know what ward?"

"Orthopaedics, Room 304. Her name was Constance Caldwell."

The receptionist scrolled through a terminal behind the desk, frowning slightly.

"Bit far back for the system to hold detail," she murmured. "But I can check the occupancy logs. Hold on."

A few minutes passed.

"Yes — here she is. Room 304. Checked in for a hip fracture. Discharge scheduled... Thursday, the 9th."

"And her date of death?"

The woman paused, then clicked a few times.

"Wednesday night. The 8th."

Her tone shifted — subtle, but Annabel caught it.

"Was the discharge cancelled?"

"Not on the log," the woman said slowly. "Sometimes the system isn't updated immediately. But if she passed... I'd expect a cancellation entry."

She offered a neutral smile. "Sorry I can't give more."

"You've given plenty," Annabel said softly.

***

Outside, the wind had picked up.

Annabel stood by the car, hands tucked deep into her coat, watching a pair of leaves spiral toward the car park curb.

"You were almost home," she whispered. "Almost."

Then she opened her notebook and drew a small line under a growing list of names — each one with a *planned future that vanished overnight.*

Room 304 wasn't just a number anymore. It was a question waiting to be asked.

Chapter 11

It started, as many things did for Annabel, with a notebook and a pencil.

The living room at Honeystone Cottage was unusually quiet, even for a Sunday. Rain freckled the windows, and Persephone snored gently beside the fireplace, her paws twitching in sync with unseen dreams.

On the dining table:

- A corkboard
- A pot of tea
- Several index cards
- A long line of *uncertainty*

Annabel stared at the names she'd scrawled and pinned in a half-moon arc.

- Constance Caldwell – Room 304, hip fracture, improving
- Morris Elford – BP stabilized, no kin, discharge planned
- Nora Hensley – child, "unexpected but peaceful" death
- Glenda Marsh – cheerful and ready to go home
- Dorothy Combs – informant name corrected post-death

Each had died *at night.*

Each had *no family at bedside.*

Each had been *expected to recover.*

Annabel added another column "Seen or forgotten?" and started quietly noting whether anyone visited regularly, whether the nurses wrote "cheerful" or "difficult" and whether someone might have misunderstood solitude as abandonment.

She started with Constance.

Evie had been away on assignment. Her name wasn't listed in any hospital logs. It was entirely possible the night staff never even knew she existed.

Morris Elford — no known family.

Glenda Marsh — widowed, quiet, no one mentioned coming in.

Nora Hensley — parents overwhelmed with a second child who needed full-time care.

Dorothy Combs — staff couldn't locate relatives. No visitors.

The deaths didn't just happen at night.

They happened *in silence.*

Annabel looked at the board and felt a chill that had nothing to do with the weather.

Who decides someone is forgotten?

In the centre of the board, she wrote:

"Staff. Routine. Opportunity."

Then underlined it.

***

Later that afternoon, she slipped into the Hare & Hound — where the fire was roaring, the gossip louder, and Bernard was cleaning pint glasses with all the drama of a man polishing jewels.

She didn't ask anything at first. Just ordered her usual Earl Grey, found a quiet corner table, and listened.

"I'm telling you, they should've moved her home already," said one woman. "She's been stable for a week."

"Hospitals drag their feet. Staffing's terrible. You know Rita's still doing overnights?"

Annabel's ear twitched at that.

"Rita Hembry?"

"Aye. Quiet one. Lives near the orchard. Got those three cats she talks to like they're housemates."

"They are her housemates," said Bernard dryly.

"And she prefers cats to people. Not that I blame her."

Laughter rose.

Annabel sipped her tea, letting the thread weave itself into place.

Rita.

Worked nights.

Cleaning staff — not medical, but present.

Invisible.

And observant.

And… a cat person.

***

That evening, Annabel fastened Persephone's velvet harness (a regal affair, tolerated only under protest), and took her for one of their *"coincidental walks."*

She looped near the edge of the orchard where Rita lived, slowing her pace when she saw the lights on in the window — and the unmistakable shadow of a cat tail flicking across the sill.

Persephone meowed pointedly.

"Yes," Annabel murmured. "I know. You'd prefer to be home. But we're on a mission of diplomacy."

And with a low, encouraging purr… they approached the gate.

Chapter 12

Rita Hembry's cottage was modest and well-kept, tucked behind a lean fence lined with fading nasturtiums. There were ceramic cat statues on the windowsill and a small wind chime shaped like a paw print.

Annabel tapped once. Persephone meowed loudly, as if announcing herself.

The door creaked open just far enough to reveal Rita's weathered face, framed by short grey curls and tired but sharp eyes.

"I don't do visitors."

"I brought someone who insists she's not a visitor," Annabel said calmly.

Persephone gave a tiny, queenly trill.

Behind Rita, a large tabby appeared at the window. It meowed once and vanished.

Rita's expression didn't change — but the door opened wider.

"Come in. Don't let the long-haired one near the fireplace. She likes to set her tail on fire."

***

Inside, it smelled faintly of lemon oil, cat biscuits, and something baking. There were three cats: the tabby, a sleepy tortoiseshell cat on the arm of a chair, and a lanky ginger sprawled like royalty across a windowsill. Persephone slinked in, took one long look, and immediately climbed onto the arm of the chair beside the tortie cat.

No hissing. Just a brief nose tap.

It was, apparently, a summit of equals.

"She's got manners," Rita said. "Better than most people."

"I've raised her with standards."

They sat. Rita poured tea without asking. No sugar, no milk. Just heat and habit.

"I hear you work the night shift at the hospital," Annabel said after a few quiet sips.

"Cleaning," Rita said. "Corridors, waiting areas, sometimes wards if they're shorthanded."

"Do you remember a patient from a couple years ago? Constance Caldwell. Orthopaedics. Room 304."

Rita's eyes narrowed slightly.

"Talked to herself while pruning imaginary roses. Had a hip pinned. Wanted to go home."

"She died the night before her discharge."

"So, they said."

"Did you see her that night?"

Rita paused. One of her cats jumped onto her lap, and she stroked it slowly.

"Did my rounds around three. Her door was closed, light off. Nurse said she'd gone to sleep early."

"What nurse?"

"Night staff rotates. Could've been Cara. Or the tall one with the birthmark, always on her phone."

"Did anything seem… strange?" Annabel asked gently.

Rita paused.

"That nurse," she said, "I've seen her before. Not just once. A few months ago. Same shift. Another one died. Different ward — Cardiology, I think. Also due to go home. No visitors."

Annabel tilted her head slightly.

"You remember that?"

"I remember the puzzle book on his tray," Rita said. "He was finishing a crossword during my round. Light off an hour later. Found cold in the morning."

She took a long sip of tea.

"No alarms. No panic. Just… gone."

Annabel felt her pencil twitch in her bag, wanting to write that down.

"And the nurse?"

"Same walk. Same perfume. The kind that tries to cover tiredness. She's there, and then she's not."

"Do you know her name?"

"No badge," Rita said. "Never wears one. Tall. Brown hair. Something clipped at her collar. Quiet voice."

Annabel nodded slowly, the image forming.

"You've seen more than you realize."

"I clean," Rita said. "It's my job to notice what's been left behind."

A silence fell between them, heavy but not uncomfortable.

Annabel sipped her tea and looked at Persephone, who was now curled up with the tortie like they'd been born under the same moon.

"Do you remember what was left behind?"

Rita didn't answer for a long time.

"Caldwell's tea mug," she said finally. "Still had a half biscuit on the plate. The other patient's Sudoku book was open. He'd just started a new puzzle."

"And no alarms were raised?"

"They were found in the morning," Rita said, setting her cup down. "Because no one was looking before that."

Annabel nodded once.

"Thank you."

"I didn't say anything useful."

"You did," Annabel said. "You said more than the system ever could."

Chapter 13

The rain had picked up again, tapping against the windows in erratic bursts. Annabel had just finished rearranging two notes on her corkboard — shifting Dorothy Combs and Glenda Marsh slightly, trying to draw clearer lines between dates and ward locations.

She didn't hear the door open — Persephone did, her ears flicking sharply.

"Back door was open," Evie called from the kitchen. "I brought that lemon drizzle you like."

Annabel turned, smiling faintly. "You're a saint."

"Hardly. I stole it from a meeting I didn't want to attend."

She stepped into the room, brushing rain off her jacket. Persephone weaved around her ankles, then darted toward the board with her usual curiosity.

Evie froze.

Her eyes locked on the name tacked to the centre-left of the corkboard.

CONSTANCE CALDWELL

Age: 68

Discharge: Scheduled

Died: Overnight

Visitors: None listed

Evie didn't speak.

Not at first.

She crossed the room slowly and stared at the card. Her mouth tightened. Her hands clenched and unclenched by her sides.

"You put her name on the board," she said, flatly.

"Evie—"

"No. It's fine." Her voice cracked on the word 'fine.' "She belongs there, doesn't she?"

Annabel hesitated. "Only because she fits the pattern."

"Because someone *thought* she was alone."

Annabel didn't move.

Evie's eyes glistened, but she blinked it back.

"I wasn't there. I was in bloody Brighton chasing a rainstorm that never came. I told her I'd be back Thursday. She died Wednesday night."

A bitter laugh. "That's practically poetry, isn't it?"

"Evie, none of this is your fault."

"Doesn't matter." She wiped at her eyes, roughly. "She thought I'd come. I didn't. So, someone — someone — thought *she had no one.* That no one would ask questions."

She took a deep breath.

"Well, I'm here now."

Persephone nudged against her leg, silent but insistent.

Evie looked at the board again.

"Whoever did this… they think they're clever. Quiet. Surgical."

Her eyes narrowed. "But they missed something. They missed *me*."

Annabel watched her closely.

"You want in?"

Evie's answer was instant.

"Hell yes."

She grabbed a pen from the table and stabbed it toward the board.

"So, where do we start?"

Chapter 14

Evie showed her old press ID at the front desk with a confidence that didn't allow for doubt.

"Evie Heath, freelance. Doing a piece on volunteer programs in rural health systems — should only need a few quick quotes."

The receptionist looked tired and uninvested.

"You'll need to check in with someone from Admin."

"Already did," she lied smoothly. "They said I could start with Ward B, then loop back. Just light stuff. Human interest."

The woman waved her through with barely a glance.

***

She was inside.

The hospital felt different when you weren't grieving or carrying flowers. It had an edge to it — all the hum of machines, the click of staff shoes, the quiet boredom of waiting.

Evie moved like she belonged, her notepad half-visible in her bag and her eyes *everywhere*.

She poked her head into the volunteer nook.

Chatted up a porter about snack machines.

Scribbled meaningless notes and waited.

Waited until she saw *a nurse in navy scrubs* walk by without a badge.

Tall.

Brown hair pulled back.

Clip on the collar.

Quiet steps.

Evie followed, subtle.

***

She caught her near the end of the hall, pretending to inspect the volunteer noticeboard.

"Hi," Evie said brightly. "Do you mind if I ask a quick question?"

The nurse turned slowly. Her expression was polite but unreadable.

"Depends on the question."

"You work nights, right?"

"Sometimes."

"Have you been here long?"

"A while."

No name tag.

Evie stepped in just enough to feel like a presence, not a pest.

"Doing a feature on volunteers — but I keep hearing your name mentioned. You're the one who's always calm under pressure, right?"

A flicker. A twitch at the corner of the nurse's eye.

"I prefer calm," the woman said.

"Do you remember a patient named Morris Elford?"

A pause. Too long. Then:

"No. We see a lot of patients."

"He loved Sudoku," Evie added.

The nurse blinked. Just once.

"I really need to get back."

"Of course," Evie smiled. "But just one more—"

"I said—" the nurse's voice sharpened, just slightly. "I need to get back."

She turned and walked away — brisk, practiced, fast.

Evie watched her go; heart ticking faster than she let on.

Gotcha.

***

Back at Honeystone Cottage, Annabel was setting out mugs when the door flew open and Evie stormed in.

"She's real. Tall. Brown hair. No badge. And *she flinched* when I mentioned Morris."

Annabel stared. "You went in?"

"Would you have stopped me?"

"No. But I would've packed you a lunch."

"Next time."

She dropped into a chair.

"I think she's the link. Now we just have to prove it."

Annabel passed her a biscuit.

"Then we'd better get to work."

Chapter 15

Rita had expected Annabel or Evie.

Not both.

Annabel stood just off the porch step; Persephone tucked calmly in her arms like a furry diplomat.

Evie stood beside her — arms crossed, jaw set, eyes sharp but tired.

Rita opened the door without a word and stepped aside.

The kettle was already on.

***

They sat in silence for a few minutes — cats circling like curious ghosts.

Persephone settled beside the tortie again, and Evie scratched her ear absentmindedly, her fingers a little too tight.

Annabel finally spoke.

"Rita… I described the nurse to you. The one Evie saw at the hospital."

Rita nodded once. Her face unreadable.

"Tall. Brown hair. Clip at the collar. No badge."

Evie's voice cut in. "She didn't flinch when I asked questions. But she shut down. Like she's used to slipping through."

Rita's hands were folded in her lap, still as folded linen.

"I've seen her," she said at last. "A few times. Always on nights. Always gone by morning. Doesn't talk. Doesn't smile. Doesn't wear a name."

Evie's fingers twitched.

"Then you know. It's her."

"Maybe," Rita said softly. "But knowing… isn't the same as proving."

Evie exhaled, too sharp.

"So what? We wait for another body?"

Annabel reached out. Just a touch to her wrist.

"That's why we're here."

***

There was a long pause. The kettle clicked.

Rita rose, poured the tea. One cup, two cups, three. Her back to them as she spoke.

"My sister died in a hospital."

Evie looked up.

"Quiet death," Rita continued. "Nothing suspicious. Just… didn't feel right. Nurse said she slipped away. But I'd seen her that afternoon.

She'd laughed. Talked about roast chicken."

She turned back, slid a cup toward Evie.

"It doesn't take much for someone to go. But it takes *something*. And when people stop asking questions…"

Her voice trailed off.

Annabel added gently, "You've seen that nurse before, haven't you? Around other patients?"

Rita nodded.

"She floats. Between wards. No schedule I can trace. But I know others see her. Staff, cleaners and night porters. Some remember. Some… don't want to."

Evie straightened.

"Then ask them. Quietly. Off the record."

Rita looked at her, and something shifted.

Not quite a smile. Not quite sadness.

"You loved her," she said simply.

Evie blinked. "What?"

"Your aunt."

Evie swallowed hard; jaw tight.

"She was my family when no one else was. And someone thought she didn't matter."

Rita nodded once.

"Alright then. I'll ask around."

***

Outside, the wind had picked up. Persephone rubbed against Rita's ankles on the way out, leaving a trail of fur and quiet thanks.

Annabel glanced at her friend.

"You alright?"

Evie stared ahead.

"No. But I will be."

Chapter 16

The hospital didn't change.

Not really.

Same flickering panel in the corridor outside Ward C. Same cart that always squeaked on the right wheel. Same vending machine that hated taking coins after midnight.

Rita moved through it like a ghost with a mop and gloves.

"You've got eagle eyes," her supervisor had told her once. "Too bad no one looks up."

Tonight, she wasn't looking up either. She was *listening*.

***

She started in the staff break room.

Norma, one of the other cleaning ladies, was wrapping up her shift with lukewarm coffee and an open crossword.

"You see the tall nurse lately?" Rita asked casually.

"Which one?"

"Brown hair. Wears a collar clip. Doesn't do name badges."

Norma snorted. "The shadow?"

"Is that what people call her?"

"Not to her face. Don't think anyone's ever tried. She gives off that don't-bother-me vibe."

Norma leaned in, lowering her voice. "You know she's not officially assigned to any one ward?"

"Floater?"

"That's what they say. But I swear, she's always there *after* the weird ones."

"What weird ones?"

Norma gave her a look.

"Come on, Rita. You've cleaned up enough cold rooms."

Rita said nothing. Just sipped her own tea.

"She was there when that boy with the burns died. Everyone said he was pulling through. Next morning, gone."

Rita nodded once.

"Thanks, Norm."

***

Down in the laundry, she nudged the conversation again — soft touches.

"You ever wash linens from Room 304?"

The night crew guy, Paul, paused. "Couple weeks ago. Old lady. Still had her knitting bag."

"The nurse who called it in — tall? No badge?"

"Yeah," Paul said, frowning. "I remember her. Because she didn't touch anything. Just stood there waiting for the doctor like she was early for a meeting."

"You know her name?"

"Nope. Never signs off on anything. I've seen her initials though."

Rita looked up sharply. "Initials?"

"One of the charts. Not official. Just a note left on a clipboard before it went to admin."

He squinted, thinking.

"H.S., I think. Or maybe H.R. Something like that."

Rita's breath caught, but she kept her face neutral.

"Thanks."

***

Later, in the linen closet between shifts, she pulled out her flip phone — the kind everyone made fun of but *never failed her once.*

She sent the message without flourish.

Initials: HR. Staff says she floats. No badge. There when patients decline. Will keep digging.

–R

She didn't send it to Annabel.

She sent it to Evie.

Because *Evie didn't need softening.*

She needed fire.

And *Rita trusted her with it.*

Chapter 17

The message came through at 6:42 a.m.

Initials: HR. Staff says she floats. No badge. There when patients decline. Will keep digging.

–R

Evie blinked once, then sat bolt upright.

"HR. HR. HR…"

She grabbed her laptop and a mug of tea that had gone cold overnight.

Persephone, curled in the crook of the sofa, meowed her disapproval.

"Sorry, fluff queen. This is war."

***

She went to the hospital's staff directory first — basic, clunky, half the links broken. But it didn't matter.

Evie had journalist fingers.

She typed like the keys owed her answers.

Search: *H.R.*

Nothing.

Search: *Nursing Staff – Night Shift*

Slow, spinning.

Then: a list.

Row after row. Names. Departments. Shift leads. Relief staff.

"Come on, come on…"

Then her eyes landed on it.

Harriet Rose

Relief Nurse – Rotational Night Cover

- Assigned to: General Medical, Orthopaedics, Cardiology, Oncology
- Start Date: 3.5 years ago
- Contact: Internal Only
- No photo

"Gotcha."

Evie's heart jumped into her throat.

All the wards matched. The timing matched.

Relief nurse — that's how she'd float between rooms.

That's why no one really tracked her.

And no badge? Maybe because *she didn't want to be seen.*

She grabbed her phone and texted Annabel:

We've got a name: Harriet Rose. Check your email. You're not going to like it.

— Evie

***

By the time Annabel opened the door, Evie was already on her second cup of coffee, three tabs open, and halfway through a printed copy of the hospital's old 2021 rota from an online archive.

"Harriet Rose," she said before Annabel could even speak. "H.R. Night nurse. Rotates. No badge. The one Rita's seen, the one I saw, and I'll bet you *every last piece of lemon drizzle* she was on shift the night your board lights up."

Annabel took the mug she was handed. "You don't even like lemon drizzle."

"Exactly. That's how serious I am."

Annabel sat, flipping through the notes, quiet.

"Alright," she said. "Then let's find out *where Harriet Rose is tonight.*"

Chapter 18

The break room smelled of old coffee and leftover pasta.

Norma was gossiping about someone's engagement, and two junior nurses scrolled through their phones with practiced boredom.

Rita took her usual spot near the kettle.

Same chipped mug. Same silence.

She waited until the room thinned.

Then casually, almost as if she were commenting on the weather, she asked:

"Anyone seen Harriet Rose lately?"

A spoon clinked sharply against porcelain.

One of the junior nurses — a pale-faced girl with cropped hair — looked up too quickly.

Then just as quickly, looked away.

Norma frowned. "Why are you asking?"

Rita shrugged. "Saw her last week. Seemed like she was everywhere that night."

Another nurse snorted.

"She always is. Floats through like a bloody shadow."

But the cropped-hair girl — Amy, Rita remembered now — stood.

"Shouldn't you be down by Ward E this hour?"

"Finished early."

"Then maybe best not to get involved in staff business."

Rita met her gaze.

Amy's smile was small. Cold. *Practised.*

"Stick to mops, Rita."

No one laughed.

The microwave beeped.

Norma suddenly found something interesting in her tea.

Rita said nothing.

She rose, collected her mug, and left with quiet dignity.

But her hands… *shook.*

***

Back in the laundry corridor, she leaned against the wall and exhaled slowly.

Not a threat.

Not a scream.

Just a *shift*. A *crack*.

She was supposed to be invisible.

But *someone had noticed her noticing.*

***

That night, she sent a second message — this time to *both* Annabel and Evie.

Asked about Harriet. Told to mind my job. Something's shifting. Be careful.

–R

Chapter 19

Rita's hands wrapped around the teacup like it was a tether.

Annabel sat across from her, calm but steady.

"You've done more than anyone expected," Annabel said gently. "But I don't want your name to end up on that board."

Rita didn't smile.

"I've been invisible for years. But this? They see me now."

"Exactly," Annabel said. "So be somewhere they're not looking."

She pulled out a folded paper schedule — cleaning rota suggestions, shift rotations.

"Switch your hours. Work mornings. Float like Harriet floats. If she doesn't know where you are... she can't corner you."

Rita stared at the page.

"She hasn't done anything. Not to me."

Annabel met her gaze.

"Yet."

***

Meanwhile...

The engine was off, but Evie sat with the keys in her hand, fingers drumming.

She was parked just off the hospital's side exit, in a poorly lit pull-in meant for staff. The rain had come and gone, leaving the asphalt slick and reflective.

"Come on, come on…"

Then she saw her. Tall. Brown hair. That same clipped collar. Still no badge.

Harriet Rose exited alone. Didn't look around.

Walked with a kind of… *emptiness*.

Evie didn't move until Harriet was half a block away.

Then she slipped into gear, headlights off, and followed from a distance.

***

It wasn't far.

A quiet cul-de-sac lined with small houses.

Harriet's place was halfway down — semi-detached, all curtains drawn, lawn trimmed within an inch of its life.

She entered without pausing. Lights stayed off.

Evie parked down the street and waited.

And watched.

And waited some more.

Her phone buzzed. Annabel.

She answered quietly.

"I've got her."

"Evie—what do you mean—"

"Followed her from the hospital. Got an address. Quiet street, looks too neat. Like her."

"And?"

"And I want to knock."

A pause.

Then: "Wait for me."

"Already did. Hurry."

Chapter 20

Harriet Rose opened the door with a startled jerk, still in scrubs, hair now half-tied, a cereal bowl in one hand and a sock clinging to her elbow.

She blinked once, twice.

"What…?"

Annabel stepped forward. "Apologies for the visit. We won't keep you long."

Harriet looked past her — saw Evie just behind, arms crossed and fire in her eyes.

"I'm calling the police."

"Please do," Evie said. "You're all over the place. Literally."

"Excuse me?"

"Orthopaedics.   Oncology.
Cardiology. No badge. No ward. But
always there… when things go
wrong."

Harriet's hand hovered over the
doorframe.

"What is this? Who are you?"

"I'm the niece of Constance
Caldwell," Evie snapped. "And you
were the last person in her room."

The silence was suffocating.

Then Harriet stepped back, just
enough for them to enter.

***

The inside didn't match her
ghostly shifts.

The flat was dim, cluttered, and smelled faintly of damp laundry and stale cereal.

Stacks of unopened mail teetered on the sideboard.

Dishes gathered on every available surface.

A dusty plant drooped in the corner like it was giving up.

Harriet dropped the bowl on the sofa, nearly missing a cushion.

"I don't know what you think you're doing. But I'm not what you're looking for."

Annabel's voice was even.

"You've been present for more unexplained deaths than most senior nurses."

"Coincidence."

"Coincidences don't avoid name tags. They don't float between wards without documentation."

"No one told me I had to stay in one place. They're always short-staffed. I go where I'm sent."

"And do you do your job?" Evie asked, arms still crossed.

Harriet didn't answer.

Instead, she slumped onto the couch and rubbed her eyes.

"I… try. I guess."

"People died under your watch."

"People die in hospitals all the time."

Evie stepped forward. "They were recovering. They had visitors coming. They weren't ready."

Harriet looked up then — tired, yes. But not cruel.

Just… *empty.*

"You think that I did it?"

She gave a bitter laugh.

"If only I had that much control. Most nights I barely know what room I'm in."

Annabel sat, gently. "So maybe you didn't do anything."

"That's what I said."

"Maybe that's the problem."

Harriet blinked.

"What?"

"You didn't notice," Annabel said softly. "You didn't listen. You didn't check vitals again. You didn't stay when you could have. Maybe you didn't *do anything wrong*."

She paused.

"You just *didn't do anything*."

Harriet's mouth opened, then closed. Her fingers picked at the fabric of her sleeve.

"I used to be good at it. At nursing. I think. But everything's so loud now. And too fast. And no one stays. Everyone leaves. So, I just… show up."

Evie shook her head. Not out of anger now — just *bone-deep disappointment.*

"You don't even know what you missed, do you?"

"No."

"Then you shouldn't be there."

They stood.

Annabel turned to her at the door.

"We won't stop looking. But if you remember something — anything — you tell us."

Harriet didn't reply.

But she didn't close the door, either.

Chapter 21

Honeystone Cottage was quiet, the lamps low, Persephone curled into her favourite chair like a crown atop velvet.

Annabel stood before the board again. The names stared back at her — dates, shifts, wards.

All lines that led to the same point: *Harriet Rose was always there…*

…but never quite enough to be the one.

Evie paced behind her, mug in hand, voice low and ragged with frustration.

"If it's not her, then who the hell is it?"

Annabel picked up a pin and held it between her fingers like it held weight.

"Someone who knows when Harriet's on duty. Someone who knows the system."

"Medical staff?"

"Too obvious. Too traceable."

"So, who? Janitor?"

"Maybe. But there's another kind of person."

She turned slowly, eyes narrowing with thought.

"Someone who *used to belong here.* Or… *pretends to.*"

Evie stopped pacing.

"You think they're not staff?"

Annabel nodded.

"I think they used to be. Or were close enough to be trusted. Maybe someone *with medical knowledge* — but *without supervision.*"

Evie frowned. "Like a first responder?"

"Or a volunteer. A former medic. A family member who knows the layout. Someone who *blends in by routine.* Who slips into the hospital the way we slip into the village shop."

She stared at the board again.

"What if they're not on the roster… *because they're not supposed to be.*"

***

The next morning, at the Hare & Hound, Evie was tearing into a warm croissant like it had personally insulted her when Bernard dropped by their table.

"You two still digging into that mess at the hospital?" he asked casually, pouring tea like nothing was out of place.

Annabel raised an eyebrow. "What have you heard?"

"Only that someone's been asking around about nurses. And cleaners. And floaters."

He leaned closer. "You might be better off talking to that fellow who's always around there."

"Which fellow?"

"Dunno his name. Older guy. Real polite. Bit formal. You know the type. Been coming to the hospital for months now — reckon he's got a wife or sister on a long-term ward."

He waved a hand vaguely. "Anyway. Always see him reading by the windows. Same bench. Even the staff nod at him like he belongs."

Evie and Annabel exchanged a glance.

"Do you know what he looks like?" Annabel asked quietly.

"Grey hair. Walks with a bit of a limp. Always carries a messenger bag. Wears a scarf even when it's hot. Says he likes to keep the chill off."

Evie's hand tightened around her fork.

"Thanks, Bernard."

"No trouble." He winked. "You two always get there in the end."

Chapter 22

Hospitals always hummed, even in their quietest corners.

But the cafeteria at mid-afternoon was *barely breathing* — just the low buzz of vending machines and the occasional murmur of staff grabbing a late tea.

Annabel and Evie stepped inside like they had a reason to be there.

And maybe they did.

They didn't need to ask where he sat.

They just... *knew.*

***

He was in the corner by the window.

A small table to himself.

A paperback novel folded neatly beside a chipped paper cup.

Messenger bag under his chair.

Grey scarf wound precisely around his neck, though the day was warm.

He looked up as they approached and smiled — like they were old friends whose names he'd almost remembered.

"Are you looking for someone?" he asked, voice calm, almost… rehearsed.

Annabel stepped forward first.

"Just passing through. It's quiet today."

"It usually is, just after visiting hours," he replied. "You've just missed the rush."

His accent was local, but soft. Gentle.

Evie hovered a step behind, eyes narrowing slightly.

"You work here?"

"No, no. My wife was in long-term care here... a while back." He gestured toward the window. "I just never got out of the habit of coming by."

He smiled again, and it was perfectly timed.

"They call me Mr. G. I sit here. Drink too much vending machine tea. Keep out of the way."

"Do you still have family in the hospital?" Annabel asked gently.

"No," he said simply. "No one left."

The silence that followed wasn't heavy.

It was hollow. *Like the inside of something already emptied.*

He glanced at Persephone, tucked into Annabel's carrier.

"Beautiful animal. Therapy cat?"

"Sort of," Annabel said.

Persephone gave the man a long, unblinking stare.

And then turned away, tucking herself out of view.

***

They made their goodbyes. He smiled again.

Polite. Warm. *Impeccably normal.*

And as they walked back toward the main corridor, Evie leaned in.

"His voice is nice," she said.

"It is," Annabel replied.

"But his eyes…"

She shivered.

"They don't match his face."

Annabel didn't answer.

She was still thinking about the fact that *he never asked who they were visiting.*

Chapter 23

Annabel had learned something important over the years:

People were *happiest repeating what they believed they already knew.*

Ask the right question in the right tone, and they'd *fill in the blanks for you.*

It was just a matter of collecting the blanks.

***

She started at reception.

"You've seen the man with the scarf, yes? Mr. G?"

The receptionist smiled. "Oh yes, he's lovely. Always here. Helps visitors find their way sometimes. A bit like a fixture."

"Do you know his full name?"

Pause.

Frown.

"No, I… I thought he was with palliative. Or maybe mental health? He's always reading."

***

Annabel chatted with a junior nurse at the coffee machine near orthopaedics.

"You mean the man by the window? With the grey scarf?"

Nod.

"He used to visit someone in oncology, I think. Or maybe not. Been a while."

"Do you know his name?"

"Doesn't wear a badge. I figured he was a retired staff member."

Annabel smiled politely. "So, no one knows for sure?"

The nurse shrugged. "He's just… always here."

***

Meanwhile, Persephone was pouting in her soft carrier.

Annabel had brought her in for the children's reading hour, but things had taken a different turn.

When the leash slipped unnoticed, no one saw her roam around the side hallway toward the old vending alcove.

No one, except a cleaner, who gave her a scratch behind the ears and muttered, "Well, hello, Queenie."

Persephone sat down beside a worn cloth bench, tail swishing.

Then stared — intensely — at the corner underneath.

***

Annabel noticed the missing leash first.

"Oh no—Persephone?"

She found her ten minutes later, regal and unbothered, sitting beside something barely visible in the gloom.

Persephone sat near the vending alcove, her tail flicking with quiet purpose.

Annabel strode quickly over.

Before scolding, she noticed what the cat was hovering beside: a slim, dust-covered book half-tucked under the bench.

She reached down and slid it free.

The cover was matte, slightly warped with age.

No markings on the outside.

No hospital library sticker.

No barcode.

She slipped it into her bag.

"We'll take a proper look at it at home," she whispered.

Persephone stretched out a paw, as if giving final approval.

***

Back at Honeystone Cottage, Anabel left the book untouched on the sideboard for the rest of the day.

It wasn't until the village fell into night's hush that Annabel returned to it.

She felt tired though and decided that…would have to wait for tomorrow.

Chapter 24

The cafeteria was empty again when Annabel returned the next morning.

Evie had opted to dig through hospital structure and staff rosters, but Annabel? She followed her instincts.

Or rather… Persephone's.

The cat tugged gently on her leash, then sharply to the left.

They veered off the main corridor, past the vending alcove and the bench sagging from years of leaning visitors.

There, nestled in the shadows, something crinkled beneath Persephone's paw.

Annabel crouched, reaching down.

A small folded slip of thick paper.

She opened it carefully.

"The quietest mercy is the one no one notices."

— M.F.

Her heart thudded once, heavy.

No context. No date. No full name. Just the echo of intent.

Persephone circled her ankles, tail high, satisfied.

"You, brilliant creature," Annabel murmured.

***

Later that afternoon, she met Rita behind the hospital café with two takeaway cups and a breeze in the air.

"Have you ever heard of someone by the initials M.F.?"

Rita tilted her head. "Not sure. No ward badge?"

"No. Just… an impression. Something I found."

Rita looked out toward the courtyard.

"There's the man who sits near the window — scarf, grey hair. Always reading. Quiet."

Annabel's breath caught.

"Do you know his name?"

"Never asked. Just seemed… like he belonged. You know? Like a fixture."

"Do you think anyone else knows?"

"Funny thing is, I've never heard anyone call him by name. But he's always there."

***

That evening, Annabel returned to Honeystone Cottage and finally reached for the book that had sat on the sideboard since Persephone led her to it.

"The Art of Dying Well – A Guide to Good Endings"

She opened the cover. Nothing on the outside.

But then… there it was.

A single, faint nameplate handwritten inside:

This book belongs to: Malcolm Frayne

She blinked. The initials.

Then she flipped forward — slowly. Midway through the book, one passage was underlined, deliberate and light.

"To end pain is not to kill, but to lift."

And beneath it, a small pencil mark:

M.F.

Annabel sat still.

The quote.

The note.

The eyes from the window seat.

Everything was starting to line up.

Behind her, Persephone hopped onto the windowsill and stared into the night, tail still.

And Annabel whispered aloud the name for the first time:

"Malcolm Frayne."

***

The Hare & Hound was warm with the scent of ale, roasted nuts, and three different arguments about potatoes.

Evie slid into the corner booth where Annabel waited, Persephone snoozing beside her like a feline loaf on the banquette.

A half-drunk pot of tea steamed quietly between them.

"Alright," Evie said. "You sounded spooky on the phone. What've you got?"

Annabel opened the book carefully, the aged spine creaking.

"I found this under the bench where our scarfed friend usually sits."

She slid the folded note across the table.

Evie read it aloud.

"'The quietest mercy is the one no one notices.'"

Her voice lowered. "M.F."

Annabel nodded.

"Now look inside."

Evie flipped to the front.

"Malcolm Frayne."

She paused. "So, the initials match. You think it's the man by the window?"

"I think it's more than that. I think he's watching the hospital because he already knows it. Too well."

"And you think he's tied to the deaths?"

"I don't know yet. But we have to treat him like a serious possibility."

Evie leaned back.

"You want to do a stakeout."

"I want to know what he does when no one's looking."

"This time, let's not be the ones looking alone."

***

From the bar, Bernard wandered over with a tray of two custard tarts and one nose for good trouble.

"Did I hear you mention Malcolm Frayne?"

Annabel blinked. "You know the name?"

"Course. Everyone in this village knows everyone… or at least their groceries."

"Frayne's the one living in that overgrown cottage past the orchard.

Doesn't come into town often. Bit of a ghost, really."

"People says that he buys plain crackers, no butter. Always pays exact. Never smiles. Looks at you like you're already behind glass."

Evie: *"Charming."*

"Some people carry quiet like it's a weapon," Bernard said, tapping the table once. "Be careful with that one."

***

That night, after tea was replaced with strong coffee, Annabel called PC Tom Oakes.

"I need to ask a favour, Tom."

She told him about the man.

The quote.

The pattern.

"I'm not saying he's guilty of anything. But I believe he's not who people think he is."

"You want backup?"

"Just an extra set of eyes. You'll know what to look for better than we will. But keep it low. Please."

Tom didn't hesitate.

"Send me the name and where you'll be."

"Tilney Lane. The old cottage."

Chapter 25

It was dusk when Annabel pulled the car onto the gravel lay-by near Tilney Lane.

Persephone sat in the backseat, watching the world with the expression of someone who'd been mildly inconvenienced by an unspeakable cosmic wrong.

Evie twisted in her seat, eyeing the narrow, hedged road.

"So, this is it? The creepy old cottage in the woods. Classic."

Annabel nodded, her hands still resting lightly on the steering wheel.

"Bernard said it was the one past the orchard. He hasn't been seen much in town."

"And we're just… watching?"

"For now."

***

PC Tom Oakes arrived ten minutes later in a nondescript car that matched the hedgerows in its commitment to invisibility.

He stepped out, approached the window, and crouched by the passenger side.

"Ladies."

"Thanks for coming," Annabel said. "Off the record."

"Still not sure what I'm looking for."

She handed him the folded note.

He read it once. Then again.

"'The quietest mercy is the one no one notices.'"

He exhaled. "That's… something."

"It's the tone," Annabel said. "Not a threat. Not a confession. But intent."

"And he's always there?" Tom asked. "At the hospital?"

"For months. Maybe longer."

Evie leaned out slightly.

"We're not kicking down doors. We just want to see if he moves… how he lives… if it lines up with the kind of man who slips through cracks."

Tom nodded. "Alright. I'll loop around. Stay in the trees."

***

The cottage itself was half-swallowed by ivy and time.

It was the kind of home you inherited from an uncle no one liked and never talked about again.

One light was on upstairs. Another flickered faintly near the kitchen.

The curtains were drawn. All but one.

Annabel watched the window through binoculars.

Evie chewed on a granola bar like it might be poisoned.

"Nothing," Evie muttered. "No movement. No…"

She stopped.

"Wait."

A shape moved inside — slowly. A tall figure, carrying something rectangular under one arm.

He passed the window. Did not look out. Did not stop.

Tom's voice came through softly on Annabel's phone.

"I've got him. He's pacing. Like he's waiting. Looks… focused."

"On what?" Annabel asked.

"I don't know," Tom replied. "But I get the feeling he's not alone."

Then Persephone — curled and quiet in the backseat — sat up.

Her ears flattened.

She hissed.

Not loudly. But *directed*.

Toward the trees.

Annabel froze.

"Did you see something?" Evie asked.

"No."

Annabel turned her head slowly, eyes scanning the shadows behind them. A faint rustle. A rabbit?

A man?

She didn't know.

But she did know one thing:

When she looked back toward the cottage…

Malcolm Frayne was in the window.

Staring straight at them.

Still. Pale. Eyes blank as the glass in front of him.

And then… he smiled.

***

"He knows," Evie whispered.

"He's always known," Annabel replied.

Chapter 26

The cottage was silent.

The same hedges leaned in around Tilney Lane. The same sagging gate. But where there had once been flickers of light, shifting shadows, and a man watching from behind the glass, now… there was nothing.

No lights.

No movement.

The mailbox creaked gently in the wind, a single flyer sticking out like a tongue.

Annabel and Evie stood by the car as Tom approached the front door.

He knocked — firm, professional.

Waited.

Knocked again.

"He's gone," Evie said quietly.

"Or hiding," Tom replied. "But not for long."

He turned toward the windows, then to the porch light, flicked off and yellowed.

He made the call in low tones — a wellness check, precautionary.

Someone with an unexplained pattern of hospital presence, concerning notes, and no known next-of-kin.

It didn't take long for the approval to come through.

***

Tom pushed open the door with a gentle firmness, Annabel and Evie behind him. Persephone stayed curled in the car, tail thumping the seat like she disapproved of *everything*.

Inside, the air was still. Dry. Sterile.

No scent of life. No warmth.

The hallway was narrow. The floor bare.

There were no family photos. No shoes. No coats.

Every surface was clean. Not messy — but *erased*.

"This doesn't feel like someone living," Evie murmured. "It feels like someone waiting."

***

They moved carefully through the space.

In the kitchen there was a single pristine cup and saucer, an untouched loaf of bread and expired milk unopened on the counter. There was no clutter or warmth to indicate that somebody lived there.

In the hallway closet, Tom found stacks of identical grey scarves and boxes of blank plain notebooks.

Annabel paused by a half-closed door.

Tom nodded for her to open it. It was the study.

And here — finally — the chill curled in.

The desk was immaculate. But above it, pinned to a corkboard were printouts of hospital floorplans, photos of corridors and notes with times, dates, and initials.

A pamphlet from the hospital was pinned dead centre with the *Visiting hours: 9:00 a.m. – 6:00 p.m.* underlined.

Beside it, in handwritten notes *"True mercy doesn't wait for permission."*

Annabel stared.

"He was tracking it. Movement. Staff. Patients."

Tom crossed to a second door. Tried the handle. Locked.

He frowned.

"Padlocked from the outside."

Evie's voice was quiet.

"Like he wanted to keep something in."

They said nothing after that.

The quiet wasn't peaceful anymore.

It was *precise*.

***

Outside, the sun slipped down through the trees, and Persephone raised her head in the back seat, ears alert.

"He knew we were watching," Tom said finally, locking the door behind him.

"And he didn't run."

Annabel looked once toward the woods, then toward the path beyond the orchard.

"No," she said softly.

"He disappeared *exactly when he wanted to.*"

Chapter 27

The hospital cafeteria wasn't louder without him.

But something felt... off.

Rita stood at the vending machine, staring at a row of stale crisps and blinking LEDs when a nurse passed her, balancing two trays.

"You know what's weird?" the nurse said, barely pausing.

"That man with the scarf. Always by the window. Haven't seen him since last week."

Rita turned, brows lifting.

"Oh. Right. Yeah."

"I mean, I never even talked to him. But now that he's not there, it's like… something's out of place. Like someone moved the painting you never noticed — but now the wall looks wrong."

The nurse was gone before Rita could answer.

She stood there a moment longer, thinking.

Then she left the crisps behind and went looking for Annabel.

***

In the break room, over a lukewarm cup of tea, she sat with Annabel and Evie, both dressed like they hadn't left the shadows of Tilney Lane.

"Still no sign of him?" Rita asked.

"Nothing," Annabel said. "He's vanished."

Evie stirred her tea without drinking it.

"That's the problem," she muttered. "He's too good at disappearing. Too smooth. Like he practiced it."

Rita's eyes narrowed.

"Wait. The scarf man... he's Frayne?"

"Yes," Annabel said gently. "Do you know him?"

Rita shook her head slowly.

"No. But—someone said something. A few weeks back. I didn't think about it until now."

She stood abruptly, paced once, then turned.

"One of the palliative nurses — Ellie — she mentioned him. Said he'd asked about the oxygen tanks. Not just in passing. Like… he knew how they were set up."

"What did she say exactly?" Annabel asked, voice steady.

"She said…"

Rita paused.

"*'That quiet man — the one always in the cafeteria — he asked about the oxygen tanks. Said he'd once trained in palliative care.'*"

A silence fell between them.

This one wasn't peaceful.

"Why would a visitor know anything about oxygen systems?" Evie said sharply.

"Or ask?" Annabel added.

Rita whispered:

"He knew how everything worked.

And he knew who wouldn't be missed."

***

Tom Oakes stepped into the break room ten minutes later, summoned by a quiet text.

Annabel handed him a note — the original folded paper.

The quote.

"'The quietest mercy is the one no one notices,'" he read.

He nodded once.

"I'll file for a full warrant."

Chapter 28

The warrant arrived by mid-morning.

Tom Oakes met Annabel and Evie outside the ivy-swallowed cottage on Tilney Lane, his expression harder than usual. He didn't waste time on pleasantries.

"We go slow," he said, unfolding the warrant. "We touch nothing unless I say."

This time, Persephone stayed home. No one wanted her paws on whatever waited behind the locked door.

***

Inside, the cottage was exactly as they'd left it — clean, sparse, and cold in a way that didn't come from drafty windows.

The hallway at the back led to the same heavy door.

Tom slid the bolt back with a metallic scrape.

The door swung open with no resistance.

But the air behind it was… wrong.

Not musty.

Just *still.*

Like no one had breathed in here for weeks.

***

Whiteboards lined the walls, floor to ceiling.

Every inch was covered in meticulous handwriting.

Names.

Wards.

Dates.

Times of death.

Some names were circled in green.

Some crossed in red.

One had a faint asterisk beside it.

Evie stepped forward.

"These are patients."

Annabel scanned the names. Her voice was tight.

"And these three — they're all recent."

Tom read them aloud:

- Nora Linwood
- Morris Elford
- Rowena Hale

And beneath them, the final name — not circled, not crossed.

Just written, precisely:

Annabel Deighton Lennox

Evie froze.

"He had your name here?"

Annabel didn't move.

"I'm not a patient. He must see me as something else."

"A threat?" Evie asked.

"An interruption," she replied.

***

Tom moved toward the desk in the corner, beneath one of the whiteboards.

Inside a drawer:

- Stacks of notes
- Hospital schedules
- Maps of wards
- Handwritten night shift logs
- Oxygen system layouts
- Names of nurses

"He's been watching for years," Tom muttered.

Near the door, a small corkboard held only one thing:

A hospital leaflet, pinned like a specimen.

Ward: Rosewood

Volunteer Reader – Children's Wing

A.L. Deighton

("usually accompanied by a cat," scribbled in pencil)

***

Evie's eyes roamed the room, searching.

"My aunt's not here."

Annabel's gaze stayed on the boards.

"It would seem that he scrubbed her out," she said. "He doesn't keep what's finished."

Evie clenched her jaw.

"So, what's this, then? A scorecard?"

"A belief system," Annabel replied. "A ritual. Mercy, in his eyes."

She looked toward the small wooden chair placed against the far wall.

It sat alone, facing nothing.

Above it, written neatly in marker:

"Mercy must be methodical."

***

Tom stepped back and reached for his phone.

"We've got enough now," he said. "I'm calling it in."

Annabel stared at the final name on the board.

Her name.

"He knew we were close," she murmured.

"And he was preparing for that, too."

Chapter 29

The call came from a name Tom didn't recognize.

She introduced herself as Elspeth Wren, retired palliative nurse.

She'd seen the reports. She recognized the face in the newspaper. She said she didn't want headlines. She just wanted them to know *he wasn't always like that.*

***

They met her at a quiet bench near the hospice garden in Harlowe, two towns over.

Elspeth was in her seventies, birdlike in posture but firm in tone.

"You're not here to make excuses for him," Annabel said evenly.

"No," Elspeth replied. "I'm here because silence helps no one."

***

She told them about ten years ago, a young man who volunteered at a long-term care wing.

"He was odd, but gentle. Intense. Listened more than spoke. Took shifts others didn't want."

She took a breath.

"He had a friend. A man. I don't know if they were... but there was love there. Quiet, fierce. That man came in with cancer. Late stage. Malcolm stayed every hour he could."

"When it got worse... when it got cruel... he changed."

"He asked questions no one wanted to answer. About how long. About why we waited."

"He said—"

She looked down.

"He said it was kindness to stop what couldn't be healed."

Evie whispered, "And no one stopped him?"

"He didn't do anything *then*," Elspeth said. "He was quiet. But one day, the man died... and Malcolm disappeared."

***

Annabel's voice was calm.

"Did you report it?"

"Nothing to report," Elspeth said. "But I remember. Because he said something before he left."

She closed her eyes, repeating it slowly.

"'There are some endings so cruel, they make kindness look like a crime.'"

***

They sat with it for a moment.

Not pity.

Just *an ache* — for what pain can twist in the wrong hands.

"He thinks he's giving mercy," Evie said finally. "But he's stealing futures."

"And now he sees you as the one interrupting the ritual," Tom added, looking at Annabel.

***

They thanked Elspeth. She asked for nothing in return.

"Just stop him," she said.

"Before someone else starts thinking he was right."

Chapter 30

It was the front page of the Suffolk Chronicle.

Second column. No headline.

Just a stark black-and-white image and a name beneath it:

"Malcolm Frayne — Person of Interest in Hospital Investigation"

***

Tom Oakes stood by the noticeboard inside the Little Firling post office, watching reactions.

People squinted.

Read.

Murmured.

"That's the man from the hospital, isn't it?"

"I thought he worked there."

"Always sitting near the window. Didn't say much."

"Gives me the shivers now, looking at him."

***

Back at Honeystone Cottage, Annabel sat at the kitchen table, the paper folded beside her.

Evie leaned against the counter; arms crossed. Persephone was unusually still on the windowsill.

"You think he'll see it?" Evie asked.

"He already knows," Annabel replied softly. "But now he knows we want the rest of the world to see him too."

***

That afternoon, the letter arrived.

Plain envelope.

No return address.

Just her name.

Dr. Annabel L. Deighton

Inside: a single sheet of heavy paper, folded once.

No greeting. No sign-off. Just the words, written in ink too neat to feel natural:

"The final mercy is silence."

"The final kindness is erasure."

"You know why I chose you."

Beneath it, one line:

"The garden. Where it begins and ends."

***

Evie read it over her shoulder.

"Is that a threat?"

"No," Annabel said. "It's an invitation."

Tom arrived minutes later. He read the letter; jaw tight.

"What garden?"

Annabel didn't hesitate.

"The one behind Rosewood Ward. The hospital."

***

"He's going back?" Evie whispered. "After all this?"

"He never left," Annabel said. "Not in his mind."

Tom folded the letter.

"We go in quiet. Controlled. He wants a ritual?"

He looked between them.

"Then we'll end it on our terms."

Chapter 31

They prepared as quietly as the man they were hunting.

Tom Oakes arranged for plainclothes officers to shadow the garden paths behind Rosewood Ward.

The staff were briefed. No panic.

No announcement.

The garden remained open.

Benches swept. Shrubs trimmed.

A single wooden chair placed beside the fountain — a replica of the one found in Frayne's cottage.

"You think he'll take the bait?" one officer asked Tom.

"He's not coming for the chair," Tom said.

"He's coming for her."

***

Annabel arrived just after sunset.

The sky behind her was the soft mauve of fading light.

She wore no coat. No bag. No shield.

Only calm.

Evie waited nearby, out of view, wired and furious.

Persephone had been reluctantly left at home — *though she'd paced by the door for a full hour like she knew something was off.*

It happened with no warning.

A shape moved from the path behind the trellis.

Not rushed. Not hidden.

Malcolm Frayne walked into the garden like he belonged there.

No hat. No scarf.

Just his long coat and eyes that didn't blink often enough.

He approached the chair, didn't sit.

"Dr. Deighton."

"Mr. Frayne."

"You've made quite the performance of something meant to be private."

"You made mercy a public ritual," she replied. "You don't get to choose who notices anymore."

He tilted his head, studying her.

"Do you believe I hate you?"

"No," Annabel said. "I think you believe this was your story. But people kept interrupting the script."

"Morris Elford was recovering," she continued.

"Nora Hensley wasn't alone. You chose them because you thought no one would argue."

"And me?" she asked, voice low.

Frayne looked at her, unflinching.

"You were too close. You would have unravelled the thread. It's easier to silence before it frays."

***

She stepped forward.

"Mercy doesn't erase. It witnesses.

What you did wasn't gentle. It was cowardly."

His fingers twitched at his sides.

"They were in pain."

"And some were healing."

"Pain returns," he whispered.

"Even after hope. Especially then."

***

Behind the hedge, officers moved.

Tom stepped into view slowly.

Frayne didn't run.

He simply turned toward the fountain, breathing deeply, like he'd rehearsed this moment a thousand times.

"There's no peace left," he said.

"Not for you," Annabel replied. "But for them — yes. Finally."

***

He turned, hands out.

"Then let it be finished."

Tom cuffed him gently.

Frayne didn't resist.

As they led him away, he looked once more toward Annabel.

"You saw me. Even when no one else did."

She didn't respond.

***

Evie stepped beside her as the garden emptied.

"That was it?"

"That was him," Annabel said. "Just quiet. All the way through."

Epilogue

The days had grown cooler.

The last of the dahlias outside Honeystone Cottage bowed in the breeze, holding on just a little longer. Inside, the kettle was whistling, and Persephone sprawled in the sun-warmed patch of floor, one paw lazily flexing with approval.

Annabel poured tea without speaking.

Evie sat at the kitchen table, a small envelope in front of her.

"Tom sent it this morning," Annabel said softly while sitting across from her.

Evie opened the letter with steady hands.

"Seven confirmed. That's what the investigation thinks now. Maybe more. All timed with Frayne's presence."

"My aunt's death fits the pattern. Same shift. Same nurse. No warning."

Her voice caught, but only for a moment.

"He didn't write her name on the board."

"But he remembered her. I know it."

***

Silence settled.

Persephone blinked up at Evie, then padded over and curled at her feet.

Evie reached down and stroked her fur, once, twice.

"She wasn't forgotten," Evie said. "Not anymore."

Annabel stirred her tea.

"There's still grief," she said. "But now, there's truth, too."

***

They sat together in the quiet — not haunted anymore, just *holding space* for everything that had been unearthed.

Outside, the wind rustled the last of the summer leaves.

And in the garden, the rosemary had started to bloom again.

"For remembrance," Annabel said, half to herself.

Evie smiled.

"And for justice."

Coming Soon: Murder Sealed in Silence

A Little Firling Mystery – Book Ten

When a fierce storm tears through the sleepy village of Little Firling,

it unearths more than just broken walls and flooded fields.

Beneath the ruins of Hollowdene House — long abandoned, long whispered about — lies a secret sealed tight in stone.

A silent crime buried for decades.

A boy the village forgot.

Professor Annabel Lennox Deighton, Evie Barnes, and the indomitable Miss Persephone find themselves at the heart of a mystery that refuses to stay silent — a mystery that demands to be heard.

Because some doors were never meant to be closed.

And some voices — no matter how long buried — will always find a way back to the light.

Little Firling holds its breath again.

And this time, the past won't be quiet.

About the Author

Belinda writes layered mysteries where memory lingers, landscapes remember, and silence speaks louder than words. Her stories slip between the literary and the intimate—part atmospheric suspense, part quiet reckoning. Rooted in a love for islands, history, and hidden truths, her work invites readers to linger in the in-between.

She believes some lands carry echoes of everything they've witnessed—grief, joy, betrayal—and that nostalgia for a place is its own kind of story.

She also writes heartfelt children's stories that whisper courage into quiet hearts. With magical ladybugs, story-saving oaks, and brave little girls like Maia, Belinda hopes to help young readers find their own voice— and use it boldly.

When she's not writing, Belinda tends to her garden, guided by the rustle of leaves, the smell of earth, and the quiet company of two cats who always seem to know more than they let on.